GW00734380

THIS BOOK BELONGS TO

PUFFIN BOOKS

Published by the Penguin Group
Melbourne • London • New York • Toronto • Dublin
New Delhi • Auckland • Johannesburg • Beijing
Penguin Books Ltd, Registered Offices: 80 Strand, London WC2R 0RL, England
Published by Penguin Group (Australia), 2013

Printed and bound in Australia by Griffin Press
National Library of Australia Cataloguing-in-Publication data available.
ISBN 978 0 14 330743 3

puffin.com.au
ouraustraliangirl.com.au

Ruby and the Country Cousins

It's 1931, and Ruby and her family have lost everything in the Great Depression. Leaving behind her dad, her school friends and all that she knows, Ruby must move to Kettle Farm to stay with her cousins. Life in the country is new and strange, and Ruby has never felt like such an outsider. Thankfully she has her much-loved dog, Baxter, for company – until he gets up to mischief, and everything goes horribly wrong . . .

Follow Ruby on her adventure in the second of four stories about a happy-go-lucky girl in a time of great change.

Puffin Books

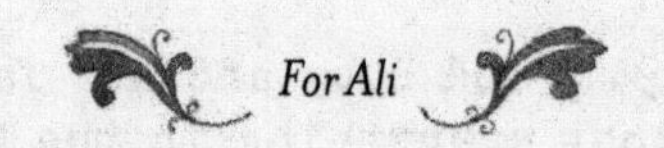

For Ali

OUR AUSTRALIAN GIRL

Ruby and the Country Cousins

Penny Matthews

With illustrations by Lucia Masciullo

Puffin Books

AUSTRALIA
1931
Darwin
North Australia
Central Austral
Western Australia
Sout
Perth
RUBY'S STORY
Will Ruby's comfortable life change forever?
Share in her adventures as she discovers
happiness in a time of great hardship.

Queensland
ustralia
Brisbane
New South Wales
Adelaide
Sydney
FCT
Victoria
Melbourne
Hobart
Tasmania
Where this story takes place
N
S
W
E

Ruby Quinlan lives in a beautiful big house in Adelaide, with her parents and her much-loved fox terrier, Baxter. Times are hard, and Ruby knows that lots of people are losing their jobs, but her own life seems comfortable and secure.

It's a huge shock for Ruby when her father is declared bankrupt. Now Dad has sold their house to his business partner, Donald Walker – which means that Brenda Walker, the most insufferable girl in school, will be sleeping in Ruby's bedroom! Worst of all, Ruby and Mother must leave Dad behind in Adelaide and move to the country to live with relatives. For the first time, Ruby will find out what it's like to be poor . . .

1
THE LAST DAY

RUBY Quinlan stood in the garden and looked back at her house. Ever since she could remember, she had curled up in its window seats and snuggled down in front of its fireplaces and played hopscotch on its wide tiled verandah. When she was very little she'd tried to catch the sunbeams streaming through the coloured glass around the front door, because Dad had told her they were fairies.

The house was a part of her life, a part of *her*. And now it belonged to the Walkers. Dad's building business had failed and he'd had to sell the house to raise money. Ruby knew it wasn't Dad's fault. Mother had explained to her that Australia was in the grip of something called The Depression. People everywhere were struggling because there wasn't enough money to go around.

Ruby hated what had happened to her family. By tomorrow her home would be Brenda Walker's home, and she and Mother would be living way out in the country with their relatives, the Camerons.

Although Aunt Vera was her mother's older sister, Ruby didn't really know the Camerons. The last time she'd visited their farm she was six years old, and the only thing she remembered about it was being pecked by a rooster. She and her cousin May were the same age, so they should have been good friends, but they weren't. May was actually rather odd. All Ruby's friends had thought so when they met her at Ruby's twelfth birthday party last year.

As Marjorie Mack had said later, she'd stuck out like a cabbage in a rose garden.

Right now Ruby didn't want to think about May Cameron. Her plan was to take some special 'last day' photographs of her home. She might even get them framed. Dad had framed some of his best work.

Standing near the front gate, she adjusted her camera until she had the perfect image. In the camera's viewfinder the house was no bigger than a postage stamp. If only she could shrink the real house to this size and keep it forever, like a precious jewel! If only –

'Hello, Ruby.'

Ruby nearly dropped her camera. Oh my hat, she thought, turning around. It's Brenda Walker. I wish she wouldn't sneak up on me like that.

'Shouldn't you be at school, Brenda?' she asked.

'Miss Fraser sent me home early because I

was feeling sick. The nurse said I might have a touch of colic.'

'And do you?'

'I don't know.' Sunlight flashed on Brenda's round spectacles. 'Actually, I came by specially to say goodbye. Are you very excited?'

'No.'

'Why not? You're going to live in the country! You might have your own horse!'

'Nobody ever said anything about a horse.'

I don't even have my own bicycle any more, Ruby thought. How can Brenda stand there and talk to me as if I'm going on some sort of amazing adventure? Can't she understand that I've lost practically everything, and I have to live somewhere I absolutely don't want to be?

She re-aimed her camera, tripped the shutter, wound on the film, and walked back down the path.

Brenda followed her. 'You could take a photograph of me,' she suggested.

'I'm only taking photographs of things I want to remember,' Ruby said. 'You'd better get on home, Brenda. You might start feeling sick again.'

'I suppose I might. I'll say goodbye, then. Goodbye, Ruby.'

'Goodbye, Brenda.'

Ruby waited until she heard the front gate click shut, and then she photographed her little fox terrier, Baxter, who was happily killing an old slipper of Mother's beneath the wisteria arbour. Next she photographed the fishpond with its fountain, and the shiny green ceramic frog that lived in the rockery. Ruby had given the frog to Dad for his birthday only last year.

It broke Ruby's heart that Dad couldn't come to the country with her and Mother. He had to stay behind to try and find work and to help with the sale of all the things the Walkers didn't want. 'Odds and sods' the auctioneer called them, as if they were just rubbish.

Ruby took a photograph of the front door, leaving just one exposure on her roll of film, and went back inside the house. She found her father in his study, taking his framed photographs off the wall.

'I don't know if anybody will want these,' he said. 'But the frames could be worth a few bob.'

Ruby was shocked. 'Dad, you can't sell your photographs!'

'We have to make as much money as we can from this sale, sweetheart. The men who used to work for me have wages due to them. Why should they suffer because I couldn't run a business properly?'

'You did run your business properly! You didn't do anything wrong! You're the best builder in Adelaide!'

'I wish I could believe that.' Dad placed the last of the photographs on the pile.

Ruby put her hands over her mouth to stop herself from saying anything more. She wanted to scream about the awfulness of what was happening, but Mother had told her that Dad mustn't be upset – he already had such a lot to cope with. So instead she made herself look at the photographs. 'I love these. Will it be all right if I take just one?'

'I suppose so. Take whatever you want.'

One by one, Ruby picked up the black-and-white photographs. They were nearly all of country scenes – hills in cloud shadow, a wheat field, a ploughed paddock with a flock of birds.

'They're smashing, Dad, honestly. Do you think I'll ever be as good as you are?'

'Of course you will. Photography is a wonderful hobby, and it's something we can enjoy together when...when money isn't a problem for us anymore. I want to see some beautiful work from you. You'll be living in a lovely spot, so you should find plenty of inspiration.'

Lovely? I'm sure it isn't a bit lovely, Ruby

thought. She looked at the photographs again, and chose a picture of an old stone building nestled under a tree on the side of a hill. Dad had photographed it in low sunshine so that every detail was outlined in glowing light. 'I like this one,' she said.

'It's yours.'

Ruby hugged it to her chest. 'Dad, do you remember how when I was a baby you told me the coloured sunbeams in the front hall were fairies? I really believed you. I knew you'd never tell me a fib.'

'Perhaps they were fairies. Who knows what fairies look like?'

'I do. They look like little coloured lights.'

Dad smiled. Then, serious now, he sat in his chair and looked up at her. 'Ruby, I know I've failed you and your mother. I'd give anything to make it all right again. But whatever happens, remember that I love you. I love you very much.'

Ruby felt her spine prickle. 'Dad, do
things like that. It scares me.'

'I'm sorry, sweetheart. The last thing I mean
to do is scare you. You're going to be all right, I know. You'll find your feet in no time.'

Ruby could see that Dad was making a huge effort to be cheerful. Her chin started to wobble, and she turned away so he wouldn't see.

'It's just that people might say things to you – about me, about what happened to my business. If they do, try not to be upset. I can't make things better for us now, but one day I will. We won't give up, will we?'

Ruby didn't dare speak. She shook her head.

'Good girl,' Dad said. 'And now I could do with a cup of tea. Why don't you ask your mother to put the kettle on?'

2

ODBYE

THEIR train was due to leave at 4.35 in the afternoon, and Uncle Donald had promised to come in his car at 3.30 to take Ruby and Mother to the Adelaide Railway Station. He'd offered to give them a lift because Dad didn't have a car now. The Buick had been one of the first things to be sold.

Together Dad and Ruby carried the luggage – a steamer trunk, two suitcases and a round hatbox – into the front hall. Afterwards, with just a few minutes left, Ruby walked all through the house, breathing it in for the last time.

'Goodbye,' she whispered as she went from room to room. 'Goodbye, kitchen. Goodbye, bedroom.'

She went out of the house and into the front garden. 'Goodbye, fountain. Goodbye, fishpond. Goodbye, poor little fishes. I hope Brenda remembers to feed you.'

Ruby jumped as she heard the crunch of wheels on the gravelled drive, and the *beep-beep* of a car horn. This is it, she thought. She felt as if she'd been emptied out and then filled up to the brim with sadness. But when Donald Walker walked towards her over the lawn she managed to smile at him. 'Hello, Uncle Donald.'

'Good afternoon, Ruby. All ready for the great adventure?'

'Mm,' said Ruby. 'Come inside – there's a pile of things to carry out.'

'Right then. I'd better give Harry a hand.'

Dad was already at the front door, struggling

with the two heavy suitcases. After him came Mother, pale and calm, carrying the hatbox. Although the weather was quite warm, she was wearing her best tweed suit. Around her shoulders was a fox fur, its two ends clipped together by the fox's head so that it looked as if the animal was biting his own tail. Ruby liked to imagine that the fox was alive and could talk to her. 'Don't worry,' he said now, winking one bright glass eye. 'Don't be sad.'

In hardly any time at all everything was loaded into the car. Ruby hugged Dad goodbye, holding her breath so she wouldn't cry, and climbed into the back seat. 'Baxter!' she called.

The little dog loved going for drives. He leaped up into the car and settled himself on her lap. Ruby held him close, burying her face in his warm, Baxter-smelling neck. She wondered if he knew he was leaving home for the last time.

Uncle Donald pulled on his driving gloves. 'All ready, ladies?'

'All ready,' Mother said.

Ruby wound down the window and waved to Dad. She could hardly see him through the blur of tears, but she tried to smile. She picked up Baxter's front paw and made him wave too.

And then they were off.

Ruby couldn't help being a little bit excited by all the noise and bustle at Adelaide Railway Station. Trains hissed and sighed, clouds of steam billowed, brakes screeched, whistles shrilled. Announcements boomed over the loudspeaker.

Ruby found that she was holding her mother's hand, and Mother was clutching her hand back, hard. Baxter shivered miserably at the end of his lead.

Uncle Donald found a porter to carry

their luggage and directed them to the right platform, where their train was waiting.

'Will you be all right, Winifred?' he asked Mother.

'Perfectly,' Mother replied. 'Thank you, Don. You've been very kind. And you will look after Harry for me, won't you?'

'Of course I will. Goodbye, then. Good luck!' Uncle Donald tipped his hat to Mother, grinned at Ruby, and disappeared into the crowd.

The porter stowed their luggage in the guard's van, and Baxter, his short tail wedged firmly between his legs, was tied up beside it. The guard fixed a label to his collar that said *Quinlan – Mt Pleasant*. As Ruby walked away from him, Baxter began to whine. The sad little sound brought tears to Ruby's eyes all over again.

'Mother, please can I stay in here with Baxter?' she begged. 'He doesn't know what's happening, and he's so unhappy. Listen to him!'

'Sorry, miss,' said the guard. 'No passengers in the van.' He winked at Ruby. 'Don't worry about this little bloke. Once we get moving I'll get him a drink of water.' He reached into his waistcoat pocket and pulled out a big silver watch on a chain. 'You'd better get into your carriage, ma'am,' he said to Mother. 'Train's due to leave in less than half a minute.' Turning away from them, he blew a shrill blast on the whistle that hung around his neck. 'All aboard!' he shouted.

Ruby and Mother hurried back to their carriage. Seconds later the train gave a loud metallic screech and began to move out of the station, gradually gathering speed. Mother opened up her *Ladies' Home Journal* and began to read – as if, Ruby thought, this was just an ordinary day and an ordinary train trip.

After about half an hour the train began the climb into the Adelaide Hills. Ruby could hear the locomotive starting to chug more slowly as it built up steam. Smoke from the smoke-stack drifted past her window. The air was cooler now, and the stations were further apart.

Sleep's Hill, Blackwood, Belair, Long Gully, Mount Lofty...Slowly the Hills stations came and went. At some of the halts the guard stepped off the train to deliver a box or a package and have a friendly chat with the station master. During a long stop at the Bridgewater station, Ruby stuck her head out the window and saw a couple of ragged men look furtively around before climbing into the guard's van. Swaggies, probably, looking for a free train ride. Immediately she heard furious barking in the distance, and she couldn't help smiling to herself.

'Be nice to them, Baxter,' she murmured.

By the time they reached the branch line at Balhannah, the sun was beginning to set. There was a delay while passengers and goods were transferred to the Mount Pleasant train, and then off they went again. The train rattled and swayed. *Clickety-clack. Clickety-clack. Clickety-clack.* Soon the windows showed nothing but blackness.

3
ARRIVING

'MOUNT Pleasant!' shouted the guard, swinging himself down to the platform as the train slid to a stop. 'End of the line!'

Mother sat up with a jerk and straightened her hat. 'I must have dozed off. Good lord, it's after seven o'clock.' She began to fuss around, collecting the hatbox and her handbag and an umbrella, and looking under the seat for her magazine, which had slipped from her lap.

Ruby stood up. Her stomach was jumping with nervousness. All kinds of thoughts crowded into her head. Would her aunt and uncle be pleased that she and Mother were staying with them? What would life on the farm be like? Would she and May become friends?

She hopped down from the carriage and went to collect Baxter, who greeted her with a frenzy of happy barking. She untied him and led him out onto the platform.

In the light from the station building several people were waiting. Ruby couldn't remember clearly what Uncle James Cameron looked like, but she knew he'd be easy to pick because he'd lost an arm in the war.

A tall, thin man stepped forward. The right sleeve of his coat was empty, pinned up.

'Ruby?'

'Hello, Uncle James.'

'You've grown. I almost didn't recognise you.' He raised his hat as Mother came up to him. 'Evening, Winifred.'

'Good evening, James,' Mother said. She

juggled her bags, dropped her umbrella. 'This is most thoughtful –'

Uncle James interrupted her. 'Excuse me, Winifred, does that belong to you?' he asked, jerking his thumb at Baxter.

'He's not a *that*,' Ruby said. 'He's Baxter. He's my dog.'

'Nobody told me I'd be taking in a dog,' said Uncle James. His face twitched. 'I've got two already, and they have to work for a living.'

'I'm so sorry,' said Mother. 'I thought I'd mentioned this to Vera. It's been rather difficult…Baxter means so much to Ruby, especially now. I do hope it isn't a problem.'

'As long as he doesn't cause any trouble,' Uncle James said, giving Baxter an unfriendly look. 'Got much luggage?' he asked, turning to Mother.

'There are two suitcases and a trunk in the van,' Mother replied. She glanced at the place where Uncle James's right arm should have been. 'I'll ask the guard to help.'

'We can manage,' said Uncle James. 'The car's only a few yards away. Let's get your things loaded.'

Ruby sat with Baxter in the back seat of Uncle James's rickety old Model-T Ford, squeezed up against the pile of luggage. The Ford was a bit like a wooden fruit box on wheels. It was so uncomfortable, so different from Dad's sleek Buick with its soft, padded leather seats! These seats were hard and cracked, and the wind whistled through the side curtains, and cold air crept up through gaps in the floorboards.

The car's weak headlights made a wavering tunnel of light ahead. Twice Ruby saw rabbits hopping for safety; another time Mother gave a faint scream when a white owl flapped across the windscreen and swooped up into the darkness.

Uncle James didn't say very much. Perhaps, thought Ruby, he had to concentrate on his driving. He wasn't a very good driver: the car swerved all over the road. That could have been because he had to change the gears and steer with only one arm, or perhaps it was because there were so many pot-holes.

By the time her uncle said, 'Here we are,' Ruby was frozen stiff, and her bottom was numb. Baxter, on her lap, had gone to sleep.

Uncle James turned the car into a driveway, and the headlights shone briefly on a piece of board that said KETTLE FARM in black letters. The driveway wound up a hill until it reached a dark building outlined against the sky. It didn't look very welcoming, Ruby thought with a shiver.

A dog began to bark, and instantly Baxter woke up, bristling, and growled deep in his throat. Ruby held him close. 'Don't you dare, Baxter,' she whispered. 'Be good, or – or I don't know what will happen to you.'

Uncle James stopped the car with a lurch and a roar, dragged up the handbrake and switched off the headlights. They all sat for a moment in sudden silence and total darkness. Soon, to her relief, Ruby saw a light moving in one of the house windows, and Aunt Vera appeared at the front door, holding a kerosene lamp.

'Here you are at last,' Aunt Vera said, helping Mother out of the car. She kissed her sister on the cheek. 'And here's Ruby. Hello, Ruby.' She looked at Baxter. 'And who's this?'

'Baxter, Aunt Vera.'

'Oh. We weren't expecting you to bring a dog, but I suppose... Come inside, both of you. Did you have a good trip? Don't worry about the luggage. Walter and James will bring it in later. You must be famished.'

She led them inside and down the hallway. Their footsteps echoed on the bare floorboards. The hollow sounds made Ruby feel even more dismal. How utterly frightful, she thought. They don't have carpets or electricity. Probably they don't even have a bathroom.

Halfway along the hallway a door opened onto a big room with a dining table at one end. A hanging lamp threw a circle of light over the table, which was set for supper.

Ruby put Baxter down and unclipped his lead. Immediately he set off to explore the room, nose down, sniffing busily.

Uncle James frowned. 'That dog had better not step out of line,' he said.

'He won't,' said Ruby. 'Baxter! Get away from that curtain!' She rushed forward and grabbed his collar. 'Sorry, Uncle James. He's usually very well-behaved. Sit, Baxter!'

'Walter! May! Bee!' called Aunt Vera. 'Aunt Winifred and Ruby are here!'

A small birdlike girl crept into the room and stood there, wide-eyed. That must be Beatrice, Ruby thought. She was about three the last time I saw her. She looks as if she'd like to be somewhere else, and I know exactly how *that* feels. 'Hello, Beatrice,' she said.

'You can call me Bee if you like,' Beatrice said, shyly. 'Everybody does.' She moved over to Aunt Vera, who put an arm around her.

Soon there were footsteps in the hallway, and in came Ruby's older cousins, Walter and May.

May had grown since the last time Ruby had seen her, but even so the floral dress she was wearing was much too big for her. Ruby recognised it as one that Mother used to wear.

'Hello, May,' she said.

'Hello, Ruby,' said May. Her short curly hair was tied back with a cotton scarf, as if she was in the middle of doing housework. 'How was the trip?'

'It was all right, thank you.'

Walter, May's brother, was fourteen, a skinny boy almost as tall as Uncle James. 'Welcome to the Kettle,' he said to Ruby with a friendly grin. 'Jolly bad luck, what happened to Uncle Harry –'

'That's enough, Walter,' Aunt Vera said. 'We don't need to talk about it.'

'Oh, well, sorry,' Walter said awkwardly.

'Fool of a boy,' Uncle James said. 'Stop your blathering and help me with the luggage.'

Ruby could see Walter's face go red. Looking sullen now, he went out of the room with his father. May and Ruby accidentally glanced at each other, and then looked away again.

Bee, who had been staring at Baxter, turned her face up to her mother and said, 'He's in the *house*.'

'Hush, Bee,' Aunt Vera said. 'Both our dogs are working dogs,' she explained to Mother. 'We don't allow them inside.'

'I can never understand why not,' said a voice. 'When I was a bairn our dogs always lived with us. Good for cleaning up scraps, and better than a blanket on your bed.'

An old woman hobbled towards them. She had floaty grey hair pinned up in a bun, and she wore a long black skirt, a black shawl and old-fashioned button-up boots. In one hand, to Ruby's astonishment, she held a small black pipe.

Oh my hat, Ruby thought. She's a witch! All she needs is a broom. And she must be Scottish – she sounds exactly like Miss Macdonald, at my school. At what *was* my school.

'Winifred, I don't believe you've met James's great-aunt, Flora Cameron,' Aunt Vera said to Ruby's mother. 'She used to live on the family farm at Riverton, but when her brother Tam died the place had to be sold. It had become very run-down,' she added, in a lower voice, 'and it was hugely in debt.'

'Kettle Farm belongs to me,' Aunt Flora said, putting a bony hand on Mother's arm. 'It was left to me by my father, who owned several properties half a century ago. James will inherit it when I die. Until then he and Vera have to put up with me.'

'And it's our pleasure,' Aunt Vera said quickly.

'Of course it is,' said Aunt Flora. 'I never had any children,' she told Mother. 'No husband, either. That's why I've lived so long. Shall we eat?' She turned her piercing eyes on Ruby. The last time she'd been to the zoo, Ruby had seen a wolf prowling around its cage, and there was something in this old woman's long face that had the same look.

'Ruby, is it?' Aunt Flora said. She continued to stare at her for so long that Ruby couldn't help squirming. Was her petticoat showing? Had the train journey left her with smudges of soot on her face?

'I knew a girl called Ruby once,' the old woman said at last. 'Dreadful creature. I hated her.'

4
THE FIRST NIGHT

At the supper table the grown-ups talked about the weather, the farm, and what was happening to Australia. All of them agreed that the Prime Minister, Mr Scullin, wasn't doing nearly enough to save the country from financial ruin, and the drought was making things much worse.

'It's the war being over that's the problem for us sheep farmers,' Uncle James said. 'It was a blessing when it ended, God knows, but no more war means no more soldiers. No more soldiers means no more wool needed for soldiers' uniforms. So there's no profit in wool anymore, d'you see? I lost an arm for my country. Now my country can't support me, and that fool Scullin will put us all in the poorhouse.'

Ruby listened for a while, but soon grew bored. Nobody was taking any notice of her, so to pass the time she looked at the people sitting around the table.

Aunt Vera seems quite nice, she thought, but that scary great-aunt is frightfully rude. May isn't very friendly – I think she's ignoring me, or else she's pretending to be a giraffe. Bee looks like a mouse, nibbling away at that crust of bread. Walter's still sulking because Uncle James was horrid to him. Uncle James scares me a bit, too. He seems so angry, and he has dreadful table manners. Just look at him digging his own dirty knife into the butter dish!

Ruby knew, because Mother had told her, that a real gentleman always used the butter knife, even if he was dining alone. Dad was probably eating alone right now. Poor Dad – he'd be so lonely, missing her and Mother.

She stared down at her plate. The spread of cold mutton, boiled potatoes, bread and pickled gherkins wasn't the lovely hot meal she'd been hoping for, and she'd quickly lost her appetite. She picked through the slices of meat, cutting off bits of fat and gristle.

Aunt Flora looked at her disapprovingly. 'I don't like to see children playing with their food, lassie,' she said. 'A bit of fat never hurt anyone. A wee sheep died so that you could eat. Think about that!'

Under Aunt Flora's fierce gaze Ruby didn't dare spit out her mouthful of tough meat. After chewing it for several minutes she managed to cough the stringy lump into her hand and slide it to Baxter, who was lying under her chair. As she did so, she realised that Bee was watching her. Ruby opened her eyes wide and made a

'Don't-say-anything' face. Her little cousin responded with a shy, understanding grin.

Bottled apricots followed the cold meat, and then May brought out a plate piled with slices of sultana cake while Aunt Vera poured tea from a big enamel teapot.

'This cake is really good,' Ruby said. It was the first time she'd spoken since the meal began.

'I made it for Father's birthday yesterday,' May said.

'Oh, well done,' said Ruby. 'I made some biscuits once, but they got burnt. I think it was the oven –'

'All girls should learn to cook,' Aunt Flora interrupted, spraying cake crumbs. She pronounced 'girls' as 'gerruls'. 'I was baking bread when I was seven years old.'

'I'm a hopeless cook,' Mother said, with a little laugh. 'I suppose I've been spoilt, because for many years we had our wonderful

Mrs Traill, the best cook in the world. My own skills are very limited.'

Aunt Flora snorted. 'That's not something I'd be proud to claim,' she observed. 'And it's a poor example you set for your lassie here. You're all fur coat and no trousers, Winifred, and you'll feel the chill when the wind blows.'

Ruby could hardly believe her ears. Nobody deserved to be insulted like that! She glared at the old woman, who had now lit her pipe and was puffing smoke all over the remains of the cake.

'You may be right, Miss Cameron, but I hope I'll be able to help in some way,' Mother said bravely. 'We want to pull our weight, don't we, Ruby?'

'Pull our weight?' Ruby was still thinking about Aunt Flora's rudeness. 'Yes, of course. There are lots of things we can do. I could walk the dogs!'

Uncle James choked on his tea, and even

Walter lifted his head and laughed. 'I don't think so, Ruby,' he said.

'But dogs need to be exercised,' Ruby said. 'I don't see what's funny about that.'

'I think you'll find that our dogs get plenty of exercise,' Aunt Vera said, but she said it quite kindly. 'This isn't the city, Ruby. We do things differently here.'

'You'll be sleeping in this room with me and Bee,' May said, putting down the lamp she was carrying. 'Your mother has my bedroom now, and Walter has the sleep-out. With Aunt Flora living here, we don't have another spare.'

'I didn't think I'd have to share a room,' Ruby said, disappointed. 'We have five bedrooms at home...I mean, we *had* five bedrooms at home.'

'This room is quite big enough for three,' May said, as if she wasn't listening. 'I hope you don't snore, though.'

'How would I know if I did?' Ruby looked around the room. It contained three beds, a chest of drawers and a big gloomy wardrobe that took up most of the back wall. It was the sort of cupboard where you'd expect to find ghosts or bats, she thought. Perhaps Aunt Flora lived there during the day, hanging from a hook like an old black overcoat.

'There's plenty of space for your things in the wardrobe,' May said. 'And you can have the two bottom drawers in the chest.' She looked at the bulging suitcase on Ruby's bed. 'You've got a fair bit, haven't you?'

Ruby undid the clasps on the suitcase and opened the lid. The tightly packed clothes spilled out – nightdresses of Swiss cotton, soft woolly jumpers, dresses of silk and cotton and linen. Underneath them all was Ruby's school uniform, and right at the bottom was the pink Cinderella frock she'd worn at her fancy-dress birthday party last year. Carefully wrapped in a scarf were two of her favourite things: her camera, and the little china fox terrier Mrs Traill had given her last Christmas. It was special to Ruby because it reminded her of happier times, when kindly Mrs Traill had looked after them all.

'Oh my goodness,' said Bee, who had come in with a candlestick and perched on one of the beds. 'You've got as many clothes as a…as a *princess*!'

'You won't need them,' May said. 'We don't go to the theatre much here, and there aren't too many parties.'

Was May being sarcastic? Ruby wasn't sure. She closed the suitcase and dumped it on the floor. 'I'll put everything away tomorrow,' she said.

Walter poked his head around the door. 'Ruby, I've put your dog in the laundry. He was trying to tear down one of the curtains. It probably smells of possum, because we had one come inside the other night and it ran up the curtain before we could catch it. Dad's getting a bit upset, though, so it's best to keep him out of harm's way. Your dog, not Dad.'

Ruby was mortified. It was too bad of Baxter! 'Thank you, Walter. Um – where *is* the laundry?'

'Down the back,' Walter said. 'May'll show you.'

'It's next to the bathroom,' May said. 'You can wash if you want to, but you can forget about having a bath till next week. There are pots under the beds, and the lav is outside. I'd better show you.'

She picked up the lamp and Ruby followed her along the hall and out through the back door. At the end of an overgrown path was a small, creeper-covered wooden building. The door was open, and May's lamp shone on ragged curtains of cobweb with black spiders lurking inside. The lavatory itself was a timber slab with a round hole in it.

'Oh, it smells,' said Ruby, holding her nose. 'And how do you flush? There's no chain to pull. And there's no paper.'

May moved the lamp to show her a pile of newspaper. 'There's plenty of paper,' she said. 'When you've finished, you throw down some ash. It's in that bucket there. You'll get used to it.'

I didn't think people still lived like this! thought Ruby. What on earth have Mother and I got ourselves into?

5
THE FIRST MORNING

RUBY slept badly. The mattress on her bed was hard and lumpy, and the wire mesh beneath it sagged. The pillow was lumpy too, and although the sheets smelled fresh, the blankets were threadbare. Ruby longed for her comfortable bed at home. Then she realised that this was practically the first time she'd ever gone to bed without a goodnight kiss from Dad, and tears trickled from her eyes and soaked into the horrible musty pillow.

The unfamiliar sound of a rooster crowing woke her from a terrifying dream. She was trying to escape from an angry mob of people. The crowd was pushing her forward and she was struggling to get back and trying to call for her mother, but making no sound. Then somehow Baxter was there too, and he was being trampled by an enormous police horse, and he was whimpering with pain. He was hurt – he was dying! Baxter!

She opened her eyes. Slowly the fear drained away, but she could still hear Baxter whimpering. Where was he? Then she remembered: Walter had shut him in the laundry last night. The minute she was up, she'd go and rescue him. She realised that she'd been having her nightmare about the Victoria Square riots again – that awful time when she and Mother had been caught up in the middle of a protest march.

May, a dark mound in the bed next to her, stirred and swung her legs out of bed.

'Bee!' she whispered. 'It's half past five!' She

pulled back her little sister's blanket, ignoring her muffled protests. 'Come on,' she said in a low voice. 'It's our turn to do the milking. Walter and Mother did it all last week. You know how angry Father gets if we're late.'

'What about *her*?'

'Leave her. She doesn't have to get up. She probably never gets up till about eight o'clock anyway.'

Ruby couldn't miss the scorn in May's voice. What cheek! she thought. May and Bee wouldn't get up this early either if they didn't have to!

While her cousins got dressed in the semi-darkness, Ruby pretended to be asleep. As soon as they left, she jumped out of bed, stubbing a toe on her suitcase. She squealed and hopped around for a while, then put on her dressing gown and made her way to the laundry.

Baxter was lying next to an overturned dish that had once held water. Clearly he had spent some of the night killing a towel, which he must have dragged from the wooden clotheshorse. It was lying in tattered pieces all over the concrete floor.

When he saw Ruby, he got slowly to his feet, stretched, and wagged his tail.

'Oh, Baxter,' Ruby said, looking at the mess. 'Oh my hat. If Uncle James sees this, you're in the most awful trouble.'

She heard voices in the kitchen: Uncle James and Aunt Vera must be up. There was no time to think. In the dim light she saw a bag with the word MENDING embroidered on it hanging from a nail on the back of the door. Quickly she gathered up the torn bits of towel and stuffed them into it. She'd come back later and try to find a better hiding place.

'I should be cross with you, Baxter,' she said. 'But it's not really your fault, is it? Poor darling, you're bored to sobs. I'll let you out for a run.'

She went to the flywire back door and opened it, Baxter pushing eagerly ahead of her.

Too late Ruby saw the furry huddle of cats on the verandah.

There was a loud screech, and a scuffle. The cats leaped away in all directions, hissing and snarling. A big black cat flashed out a paw, and Baxter yelped as a claw raked down his nose. The cat streaked away. Baxter raced after it.

Ruby stood on the stone doorstep, wondering what to do. Very soon she decided that going after Baxter was pointless. Apart from that, her feet were cold and she wasn't wearing slippers.

She closed the door and tiptoed back to bed.

The chip heater in the bathroom was lit only once a week for baths because, as Mother explained, Uncle James couldn't afford to waste either water or fuel. All the water came from a bore and had to be pumped up into the house tank.

Shivering in her shell-pink rayon petticoat and matching drawers, Ruby dabbed at bits of herself, dipping her face flannel in a puddle of cold, tea-coloured water in the rust-stained basin. She didn't want to touch the large orange block of carbolic soap, which was grimed with grey streaks and smelled like tar.

How can I ever get used to this? she thought. It's too bad. I don't want to be poor. I hate being poor. I wasn't *meant* to be poor. But May calling out, 'Get a move on, Ruby!' and hammering on the door made her so cross that she forgot to be sorry for herself. She stormed out of the bathroom, her head held high.

Breakfast was porridge, served with salt, the Scottish way. 'Porridge sets you up for the day like nothing else,' Aunt Flora told Ruby. 'I hope you don't ruin it with sugar.'

'I wouldn't dream of it.' Ruby took a

mouthful of the porridge, and gagged. 'Oh… it's horrible!'

She poured herself a glass of milk and drank it to take the taste out of her mouth.

Uncle James glared at her, his face twitching. 'In this house children don't help themselves,' he said. 'If you want something, you ask for it.'

'Oh,' said Ruby, putting down her glass. 'I'm sorry. I didn't know.' Should she pour the milk back into the jug? She decided to drink it anyway.

'And you'd better mind that dog of yours,' Uncle James said. 'He kept me awake half the night with his noise. Damn thing shouldn't be in the house.'

'But he's a *house dog*,' Ruby said. Her heart began to race: she'd forgotten that Baxter was still on the loose. She remembered the ripped towel, and prayed that Baxter wasn't doing anything else that might upset her uncle. 'He's not used to living outside.'

'I'll soon get him used to it,' Uncle James said grimly.

'Don't you eat porridge at home, Ruby?' asked Walter.

'No,' Ruby replied, grateful to him for changing the subject. Why did Uncle James have to be so beastly to poor Baxter? She took a deep breath to calm herself. 'Sometimes we have Weet-Bix. Do you know what they are? You don't have to cook them or anything. You just put milk on top, and sugar.'

'Manufactured rubbish,' Aunt Flora said, looking down her long nose. 'You might as well eat sawdust. The day I don't start with a bowl of porridge is the day they'll put me in a box.'

'And that day can't come too soon,' Ruby heard Uncle James mutter.

'More tea, Winifred?' asked Aunt Vera, holding the teapot in readiness. 'Ruby, you've hardly eaten a thing. Try some butter on the porridge, dear – it really helps.'

Uncle James pushed back his chair. 'Come along, boy,' he said to Walter. 'We've got work to do. That ewe in the far paddock is still down. We'd better get her on her feet again or she'll be joining the other dead beast down by the creek. If the foxes don't get her first.'

As soon as Uncle James had gone, everyone relaxed a little. Aunt Vera and Mother had another cup of tea, and May began to clear the table.

'May, why don't you show Ruby around the farm?' Aunt Vera suggested. 'Bee can clear away.'

'I'd like that,' Ruby said, trying to sound enthusiastic. 'I haven't been here since I was little, and I've forgotten just about everything. Except the rooster.'

'The rooster?' asked Aunt Vera.

'A rooster pecked me on the leg, and it hurt a lot. I had blood on my sock.'

For the first time Ruby could remember, May actually laughed. 'That's funny,' she said, 'because we thought that while you're living with us, you could look after the chooks.'

6
KETTLE FARM

'WHY is this place called Kettle Farm?' Ruby asked May. 'It's a strange name, isn't it?'

May shrugged. 'Not really. Dad's family come from a place in Scotland called Kettlebridge. They settled in South Australia nearly a hundred years ago.' She pushed open the back door. Cats lay everywhere, snoozing in the sun.

There was no sign of Baxter.

'We've got twelve cats,' May said. 'Or is it thirteen now? Bee has given them all names.

That big black one sitting on the chopping block is the leader of the pack. She's called Gaf, after Great-Aunt Flora. Half the kittens are hers.'

Ruby was glad to see that Gaf had survived her fight with Baxter. 'What's the chopping block for?' she asked.

'Splitting kindling wood for the stove. And chopping the heads off chooks. I expect that'll be your job from now on.'

Oh no, Ruby said to herself. Oh my hat. I couldn't possibly do that! The thought made her feel slightly sick.

May walked ahead of Ruby, her bare feet padding over the dusty ground.

'That's the garage,' she said, pointing to a long brick building. 'We don't use the car very often, because petrol costs too much. There's a buggy in the garage, too, but we sold our horse.' She stopped in front of a wooden slab fence. 'In here is the veggie garden. You can help with that, too, and the milking. Do you know anything about gardening?'

'Not much. At home we had a gardener who came every week.'

'You'll learn.'

Ruby peered over the fence and saw garden beds, concrete paths, a watering can, a wheelbarrow.

'There aren't many veggies,' she said.

'It's the end of the summer harvest,' May said. 'And in case you haven't noticed, we're in the middle of a drought.' She pointed at some distant rows of trees. 'The orchard is over there, and past that it's just paddocks. The shearing shed's down by the creek.'

She marched off, and Ruby hurried to keep up. 'What's in the paddocks?'

'Sheep, mostly. And cows. We have three house cows.'

'Are the chooks there too?'

May rolled her eyes. 'You don't think we

keep chooks in a paddock, do you? Here are our dogs. The border collie is called Shep, and the kelpie's name is Sharpie.'

The kennels, shaded by a pepper tree, were surrounded by hard dry ground littered with bones and bits of fur. 'Rabbit,' May said.

Shep trotted out to the full length of his chain, wagging his plumy tail. Ruby went to stroke him, but May called her back.

'They aren't pets – we don't play with them. Dad needs them to work the sheep, so he's the only one who can boss them around.'

'Do they bite?' Ruby asked.

'Of course not. They're really smart dogs. Smarter than Baxter, anyway. By the way, where is he?'

'I don't know,' Ruby said. 'I let him out before breakfast.' She looked all around her. 'Baxter!' she called. 'Baxter!'

'He'll turn up,' May said. She kept walking. 'Here are the chooks.'

Ruby saw a large area enclosed with chicken-wire. At one end was a stand of pine trees. As May and Ruby got closer, the chooks raced up to the fence, clucking and squawking. Most of them were black, but there were several very finely striped in black and white. And there was the rooster, strutting, his tail feathers gleaming. Ruby wondered if it was the same rooster that had pecked her all those years ago. How long did roosters live?

'The black chooks are Orpingtons,' May told her. 'The stripy ones are Plymouth Rocks. They're special. We only have six of those.'

Ruby wrinkled her nose. 'Chooks don't smell very nice, do they?' she said.

'They smell like chooks,' May said. 'You'll have to feed them before school in the morning and again before supper. The grain is kept in that little shed over there.' She turned and pointed. 'You have to collect the eggs, too. We keep about a dozen, and we take the rest to the store to sell.'

May sounds just like Miss Fraser at my old school, Ruby thought. She has the same flat voice. Except that Miss Fraser turned out to be really nice, in the end.

Mother had once said that May was shy, but Ruby didn't think she was shy at all.

May just doesn't like me, Ruby realised with a shock. It was a new feeling. People usually like me quite a lot, she thought. Even Brenda Walker likes me. What have I ever done to May that she should dislike me so much?

'There's your dog,' May said suddenly.

Ruby turned around to see Baxter trotting up to her, tongue lolling, eyes bright. 'Thank goodness,' she said. 'Baxter, where have you been?' She bent down to stroke him, and then pulled away. 'Oh, you've rolled in something *bad*.'

'He must have found that dead sheep down by the creek,' May said, with a slight smile.

'You should keep him tied up.'

'I couldn't tie him up. He'd hate it!'

'You mightn't have much choice,' replied May. 'He's a town dog. He doesn't belong here.'

'You needn't think I'm going to pick you up, Baxter,' Ruby said, knotting her handkerchief to Baxter's collar as a lead. 'Poo, you really stink.'

May's right, she thought. Baxter doesn't belong here, and I don't belong here either. It's so unfair! I never wanted to be here in the first place. Why couldn't Mother and I have stayed with Dad? We'd have managed somehow.

Back at the house, Ruby dragged Baxter stiff-legged past the cats, ignoring his growling.

As she and May made their way to the kitchen, Uncle James appeared at the laundry door. He was in his shirtsleeves, his braces hanging down, his hair and face dripping wet. 'Vera!' he bellowed. 'Vera! What have you done with my towel?'

'I've done nothing with it,' said Aunt Vera,

bustling over to him. 'It should be on the clotheshorse. Oh dear, what is that smell?'

'I'll look for your towel, Dad!' said Bee. 'I'm good at finding things.' She poked around in the laundry, opening cupboard doors, checking inside the washing basket. 'Maybe it got put in the mending bag.'

'No – !' Ruby started to say, but all she could do was watch as her little cousin ran to unhook the bag from the back of the laundry door. 'I lost my petticoat once and it was put in here by mistake,' Bee said. 'Look, here's your towel! Told you! Oh...'

She pulled out a piece of the torn towel, and stared at it.

Uncle James's face began to twitch.

'I think this might be a different towel,' Bee whispered.

Uncle James grabbed it from her. 'Different towel, my foot. It's that dog again.' He turned to Ruby. 'The dog stays outside from now on.

And if he puts one more foot wrong, I'll take him out and shoot him myself.'

'Oh, James,' said Aunt Vera. 'Surely you don't mean that.'

'He's only little,' Bee protested. 'He's not much more than a puppy. You wouldn't really hurt him, Dad, would you?'

'I'll do what I have to,' said Uncle James.

Ruby stared at him in horror and disbelief. Uncle James wouldn't really kill Baxter, would he? Of course he wouldn't. He *couldn't*. She wasn't sure, though. Uncle James wasn't a normal sort of uncle.

7
GOING TO SCHOOL

THE walk to school seemed to go on forever.

'It's only three miles,' Bee said. 'Some kids walk much further than that. You'll get used to it.'

Yes, Ruby thought bitterly. Just like I'll get used to eating salty porridge, and sleeping in a sagging old bed, and having to use that horrible smelly lavatory. Just like poor Baxter will get used to being chained up all night long and sleeping out in the cold with Shep and Sparkie.

Mother had promised to keep an eye on Baxter while Ruby was at school, and Ruby hoped that would keep him out of trouble. As an extra charm against bad luck she'd put her little china fox terrier in her school satchel, along with her sandwiches. She wasn't usually superstitious, but she felt that it might somehow help to protect both her and Baxter – and Baxter, at least, needed all the protection he could get.

The early morning sun was already hot, and the day would be hotter. May and Bee walked easily along the road, taking hills and stony patches and areas of loose sand in their stride. Ruby trudged along behind them. Her good ankle-strapped school shoes were dull with dust, her stockings had started to wrinkle, and her uniform felt tight and prickly.

The cotton frocks her cousins wore were thin and faded, but they looked deliciously cool. May and Bee weren't wearing proper shoes and socks, either, just old sandshoes freshly whitened with pipeclay.

Ruby hadn't wanted to wear her school uniform, but Mother had insisted. 'You'll look scholarly,' she said.

'I don't want to look scholarly,' Ruby told her. 'Only people who go to proper schools look scholarly. Brenda Walker looks scholarly.' But Mother had looked sad, then, so Ruby hadn't said anything more. She hated it when Mother looked sad.

'How far is it now?' she called.

'About a mile,' May said, over her shoulder. 'You'd better walk a bit faster, or we'll be late.'

'I'm walking as fast as I can,' Ruby grumbled. Putting down her satchel, she took off her school tie and undid the top button of her shirt. She wished she could take off her blazer, too, but she didn't want to carry it. Thank goodness Mother hadn't made her wear her hat or her gloves! She took some quick gulps from her water bottle, and then ran after May and Bee.

Sometimes they were passed by other

children: first by three boys riding ponies, then by a girl on a fat white horse with a younger girl sitting behind her, hanging on to her waist. A boy raced past them on his bicycle, skidded in a patch of sand, and almost fell. 'You're such a show-off, Eric Weber!' May yelled at him as he wobbled away down the road, ringing his bell.

After what seemed like at least an hour, Ruby heard the distant sounds of children playing. There, finally, was the school, a small, neat building of brick and stone, with newly planted pine trees marking the fence line. In the paddock next door some boys were kicking a football.

As soon as they reached the school gate Bee skipped off to find her friends. Trying not to look as nervous as she felt, Ruby turned to May. 'Now what?' she asked.

'I'd better show you where everything is,' May said in her cool way. 'Not that there's much to see. This part of the yard we're looking at is the girls' playground. The boys have to play on the other side. If boys go into the girls' playground, they get the strap.'

'What's the strap?'

'A belting from Mr Miller. Only boys get the strap. Girls get the cane.' She led Ruby across the schoolyard and into the enclosed porch. 'There are two rooms. One is for the babies and the other is for Grade Three to Grade Seven. Miss Head teaches the babies, and Mr Miller teaches us. He's the head teacher. I'll tell him you're here.'

Mr Miller was in the main classroom, sitting at his desk on a low platform in front of the blackboard.

'Ah!' he said. 'Miss Ruby Quinlan. Welcome to our school. I expect it will be rather different from the school you're used to, but we're proud of it, aren't we, May?'

'Yes, sir.'

'We're a friendly bunch, Ruby,' Mr Miller continued. 'You'll soon get to know us. About half our students are of German descent, and that makes for an interesting mix. Are you enjoying your stay with your uncle and aunt?'

Ruby glanced at May. 'Yes, Mr Miller,' she said.

'Yes, *sir*,' said Mr Miller.

'I beg your pardon?'

'My students always call me "sir". Yes sir, no sir, three bags full, sir. Understand?'

'Yes, Mr Miller. I mean, Yes, sir.'

'Good girl. I'll soon find out what standard you've reached. Any problems? Reading and writing? Arithmetic? You'll be working towards your Qualifying Certificate, along with the other Grade Sevens.'

'I'm not very good at arithmetic…sir.'

Mr Miller smiled. 'We'll see, won't we? Your desk is in the far row, second from the front. You'll be sharing with Doris Spinks. Put your things in your desk and then take your satchel out to the porch.' He looked at his pocket watch. 'Time for assembly. Out you go, girls.'

Ruby's first morning passed in a blur. For assembly everyone lined up in the schoolyard like soldiers, standing at attention and then at ease. One of the boys hoisted the flag on the flagpole, and then, in a loud sing-song, the children all recited the loyal oath: 'I love my country, the British Empire. I honour her king, King George the fifth. I salute her flag, the Union Jack. I promise cheerfully to obey her laws.'

The boys saluted, the girls curtsied, and then everybody sang 'God Save the King'. Two of the older boys started to bang on a drum and a triangle, and to Ruby's surprise all the children began immediately to march on the spot. 'Left, left! Left, right, left!' called Mr Miller, as two lines of marching children filed into their classrooms.

Before lessons started, the teacher asked Ruby to stand beside him at the front of the room. 'We have a new student in Grade Seven,' he said. 'Her name is Ruby Quinlan.' He turned and carefully wrote her name in copperplate on the blackboard, giving the Q an extra flourish. 'Ruby comes to us from a big school in the city, so our school will be quite a change for her. You must do all you can to make her feel at home. Ruby' – he turned to her – 'do you wish to say anything?'

As everybody stared and whispered, the only wish Ruby had was that she might sink through the floor. 'No, sir,' she mumbled.

A small boy in the back row shot his hand up. 'Please, sir, why is she wearing those funny clothes?'

'They aren't funny clothes, Ernest. Ruby is wearing a school uniform, very neat and appropriate. Go to your desk now, Ruby.' He rubbed his hands together in a jolly sort of way.

'All right, then, boys and girls! Grades Three to Five, get out your spelling books. Grade Six, turn to chapter three in your history books. Grade Seven, we'll continue our work on fractions.'

Doris Spinks had freckles and a sore on her upper lip. Her frizzy brown hair was cut short in a bob.

'Are those the clothes you wore at your old school?' she whispered as Ruby sat down beside her. She fingered Ruby's blazer.

'Yes.'

'They look expensive. Did they cost a lot?'

'I don't know what they cost,' Ruby said. 'I didn't buy them.'

'Did you go to a private school? I wish I could go to a private school.'

'Stop talking, you two!' Mr Miller loomed over them. 'One more word from either of you, and it'll be the cane.'

Doris blushed and lowered her eyes.

'Sorry, sir. It was Ruby, sir. Only she had some questions, and I was helping her.'

'All right, Doris. Thank you for that explanation.'

Ruby stared up at the ceiling. I don't believe it, she thought. I've ended up sitting next to somebody who's even worse than Brenda Walker.

8

GETTING USED TO IT

It didn't take Ruby long to know all her Grade Seven classmates, because there were only nine of them. There was May, and May's best friend Lorna Seidel. There was Doris. Sitting in the double desk behind Ruby and Doris were Iris Dunn, a small, mousey-haired girl with a crippled leg, and Betty Pfitzner. Betty looked older than the other girls, and Ruby was sure her hair had been Marcel waved.

There were four boys: Eric Weber, a very plump boy called Colin Evans, and Clive Schwartz and Bob Turner. Ruby thought of

Clive and Bob as 'the big boys'.

In the recess break Mr Miller took Ruby to the stationery room and gave her textbooks, exercise books, pencils, a ruler, a penholder and a box of nibs, a compass, a setsquare and some sheets of blotting paper.

'Unfortunately all our second-hand textbooks have been sold,' he said, 'so you'll have to pay full price.'

'That's all right, sir.'

'Good. It comes to three pounds, all up.' He handed her a piece of paper. 'Give this to your fa– I mean your mother. Don't write your name on anything until it's paid for.'

Ruby loved having new stationery. She spent the whole break stacking everything neatly in her desk and washing dried ink out of her inkwell.

At lunch time, though, she had nothing to do and nobody to do it with.

'Mum said I should look after you, but

you'll be all right, won't you?' May said.

'Of course I will,' said Ruby. Sitting on a long, low bench, she watched, trying not to feel envious, while May walked off arm in arm with Lorna Seidel.

Ruby undid her package of sandwiches – half plum jam, half mutton – and began to eat, starting with the jam ones. Everybody else seemed to have someone to sit with and talk to. Doris, sitting on a patch of dry lawn with her ankles neatly crossed, was eating her lunch with a Grade Six girl called Verna Pfeiffer.

Before long the boys returned to their football and the girls started a skipping game with the long rope. In another corner of their playground some of the younger girls began to play brandy. 'Barleys!' they shrieked when they were hit. Once the dirty old tennis ball they were using rolled under Ruby's feet, and she picked it up and threw it back.

'D'you want to play with us, Ruby?' called

Bee, who was 'he'. But Ruby shook her head. She knew she'd never live it down if she, a Grade Seven, were to be seen playing with Grade Three and Four children. Still, she was glad when two little boys sat on the bench next to her. It made her look less alone. One of the boys had a pile of 'Us Fellers' comic strips, cut out of newspapers.

Ruby put her mutton sandwiches in the rubbish bin. Then she took her empty water bottle and filled it up from the waterbag hanging beside the rainwater tank. The water didn't look very clean, and there was a wriggler in it, so she tipped it out. She sat on the bench again, and watched.

Country children weren't a bit like her schoolmates in Adelaide. It wasn't just that her old school was only for girls, or that everybody there wore school uniform. Most country children had sunburned faces or freckles. They moved faster, and their voices were louder, and they laughed more. And a lot of them looked really poor. Several of the girls wore blouses or jumpers that were too tight, and skirts with hems that had been let down. Ruby could see the lines where the material hadn't faded.

The girls who were skipping were Grade Sixes and Grade Sevens. They ran in and out of the rope's long curve, singly and in pairs, chanting:

I saw a nanny-goat
Putting on her petticoat
In – side – out!

May was turning one end of the rope, and Lorna held the other end. It thudded steadily on the ground, speeding up when Lorna yelled, 'Pepper!'

Ruby loved skipping. I'll ask if I can join in, she thought. May mightn't like me, but that doesn't mean everybody else will hate me too.

As she was about to stand up, Verna Pfeiffer came and sat down next to her. Ruby smiled, but Verna didn't smile back.

'Think you're a bit flash, don't you, Townie?' Verna said.

'What? No, of course I don't.'

'Why are you wearing them clothes, then?'

Ruby sighed. 'Because it's a school uniform. And I'm at school.'

'It looks stupid.'

'No, it doesn't.'

'Does too, *Townie*.'

'Please don't call me that.'

'Ooh, so sorry, Townie. I didn't think it would bother you, seeing as that's what you are. Anyway, you can sit with us if you like. Doris says.'

'All right,' Ruby said. But I'll just do it to be polite, she told herself.

Sitting with Doris and Verna wasn't nearly as much fun as being with Marjorie and Sally and the twins, Ruby's friends at her old school. All Doris and Verna did was gossip about the other girls. They talked about their clothes, and their hair, and whether or not they had a boyfriend.

Ruby couldn't help wondering what they'd been saying about her, earlier. She was glad when Mr Miller rang the bell for afternoon lessons.

When it was time to go home, Ruby found that her satchel wasn't in the porch where she'd left it. It was May who found it at last, hidden under the woodwork bench. There was a rip in the leather, and somebody had tried to scratch out Ruby's initials, which were embossed on the front in gold. And when Ruby opened the flap, she discovered, with a horrible sinking feeling, that her little china dog had gone.

Ruby stood holding the empty satchel and

sniffed back tears. 'It's bad enough that they've ruined my bag,' she said to May. 'But there was something in it, and someone's stolen it.'

'Was it valuable?'

'Not really. It was just my little china dog, but it – it meant a lot to me.'

'If it meant a lot to you, why did you take it to school?'

I wish May wouldn't always make me feel that everything is my fault, Ruby thought.

'Does it matter?' she said. '*Somebody* has ruined my bag and *somebody* has taken my china dog.'

'Most likely it's boys teasing,' May replied. 'They wouldn't steal your dog. They've probably only hidden it.'

'But why would they want to tease me?' Ruby asked, hurt. 'What have I done to them?'

'Nothing. You're just...different. You're wearing a flash uniform and you've got a flash schoolbag. Some of the kids might think you're pretty fond of yourself.'

'You should have told me that before we left home, then.'

'I can't tell you what to wear,' May replied, shrugging.

Ruby grew hot with rage, right up to the top of her head. 'That's not fair,' she said. 'You knew what everyone would think. You could've helped me, and you didn't.'

May didn't reply at first. Then she said, 'I'm sorry, I suppose it wasn't very fair. But now we'd better get going. Bee and I have got the milking to do.'

All the way home Ruby felt angry and sad. May had apologised, but it wasn't much of an apology, and it didn't change anything. She hated the school. She hated the way her schoolmates kept looking at her, the boys laughing and the girls whispering behind their hands. She hated having to walk all the way there and all the way back: the dust got in her eyes, and she had a huge blister on her left heel.

Back in her shared bedroom, she ripped off her school uniform. Then she pulled off her school shoes and stockings and flung them into a corner.

'What are you doing?' asked Bee, coming in. 'Why are you in your undies?'

'I'm in my undies,' said Ruby, 'because I am never wearing my school uniform again. Never *ever*.'

Putting on a cotton frock, she went in search of her mother. She found her sitting on an old rattan couch on the side verandah, mending a torn pillowslip. Aunt Flora was snoozing in a cane chair nearby, a large white handkerchief covering her eyes.

Ruby flopped down on the couch. 'Hello, Mother,' she said. 'Did Baxter behave himself?'

'More or less,' Mother replied. 'He slipped his chain after you left for school, and I found him digging in the vegetable garden. I don't know how he got in through the wooden fence, but he did. Then there was an unfortunate incident with one of the cats, so I had to put him back on the chain. How was school?'

'It was utterly horrid,' Ruby told her. 'Somebody stole my china dog that Mrs Traill gave me. Everyone laughed at what I was wearing, and the girl I have to share a desk with is like Brenda Walker, only worse. Oh, and you have to pay three pounds for my books and stationery.'

'Three pounds?' Mother's face fell. 'Ruby, I don't have three pence to spare, let alone three pounds.'

'What? No! Can't Dad send you some money?'

'Your father has nothing. He has given me an allowance so that I can pay Uncle James a small amount each week for our board. That's all we have.'

'What about Uncle Donald?'

'I shall certainly not ask for charity from Uncle Donald.'

'Uncle James?' But even as she said it Ruby knew how impossible that was. Then she brightened. 'I know! I could sell some eggs.'

'Ruby, do be sensible. The eggs aren't yours to sell.'

Ruby made a face. 'What can I do, then?'

'You'll have to give it all back. I'm sure you don't need new pens and pencils and exercise books – you still have what you were using at your old school, don't you? And perhaps you could borrow textbooks.'

Ruby kicked at the floor. 'Do I really have to give everything back, Mother? It's so embarrassing.'

'It's a sight less embarrassing than being in debt,' Aunt Flora said from beneath her handkerchief. 'There's no disgrace in being poor, lassie.'

'Oh my hat,' Ruby whispered to Mother.

'I thought the old witch was asleep.'

'Witches can see with their eyes closed,' said Aunt Flora, lifting the handkerchief and staring at Ruby. 'They just pretend to sleep, so they can catch young gerruls out. Eggs, indeed.'

9

BEST FRIENDS

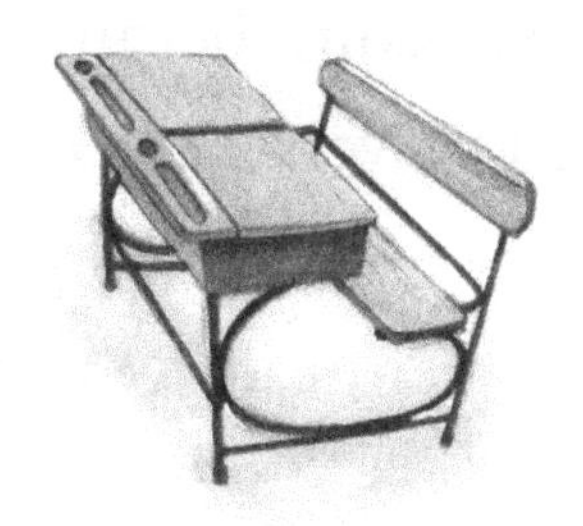

RETURNING all that lovely new stationery was one of the most humiliating things Ruby had ever done. In an instant it turned her into the sort of person other people felt sorry for.

Mr Miller was able to find a couple of dirty, dog-eared old textbooks for her, but she could hardly bear to touch them: one of them, the arithmetic book, looked as if it had fallen in somebody's greasy dinner. And later there was even more humiliation.

'Have you done much sewing, Ruby?' asked

Mrs Miller. The headmaster's wife took the older girls for sewing lessons while Mr Miller took the boys for woodwork. Everybody enjoyed these lessons, because formal rules were relaxed. 'Did you make clothes for your dolls?'

Ruby shook her head. 'No, sir. I mean, no, Mrs Miller.'

'Oh. Does your mother sew?'

'Not much. We always buy our clothes from the department stores.'

Mrs Miller clicked her tongue. 'I'm afraid you will be quite a long way behind the other girls.' She gave Ruby some squares of pale blue fabric, a needle and a wooden spool of thread, and an exercise book. On the pages of the book were pinned pieces of the same blue fabric, each one showing how to do a different stitch.

'Before you can make anything, you must learn to do the following.' Mrs Miller counted them off on her fingers. 'Tacking. Running stitch. Backstitch. Hemstitch. French seam. Cross stitch. Featherstitch. Buttonhole. Copy the examples as neatly as you can, and make sure you look at both sides of the fabric. Doris will help you, won't you, Doris?'

Ruby flicked through the pages of the book. She was very aware of Doris, beside her, breathing noisily through her mouth.

'We did all those stitches in Grade Five,' Doris told her. 'I'm making a nightdress now, see? I might do some embroidery on it, too.'

Ruby cut a length of cotton thread, licked the thread as she'd seen Doris do, and pushed the licked end through the eye of her needle. She looked over at May, who was hemming an apron. Her cousin was working quickly and skilfully, looking up now and again to compare her work with what Lorna was doing. The two friends laughed and whispered together.

Of course May is good at sewing, Ruby thought. May is good at every single thing I'm bad at. She stared at her pieces of blue fabric.

'Start with the tacking,' Doris advised her. 'Any fool can do that.'

Ruby stuck her needle into the cloth. In, out. In, out. After several minutes a line of long stitches wobbled across the lower edge.

'That's not straight,' said Doris. 'And your thread is pulling out because you didn't do a double stitch at the start.' She heaved a sigh. 'I can see I'll have to teach you everything.' She dug around in the bag hanging from two hooks at the side of her desk, and brought out a handful of sweets. All the children except Ruby had these book bags. They were made from old sugarbags, and the girls had decorated them by pulling out threads of hessian and weaving brightly coloured wool into the gaps. 'Here,' Doris said, pushing an unwrapped toffee into Ruby's hand. 'Have a lolly.'

Ruby saw that it had bits of grit stuck to it. She gave it back. 'No thank you.'

'Oh, go on! No wonder everyone thinks you're a snob.'

'I'm not, honestly.'

'Take the lolly, then. Dad works at the pub, and he gets them free.' Doris moved closer to Ruby. 'I told the other kids you can't help being a townie. Don't worry, I'll stand up for you if they tease you.'

'I can stand up for myself.'

'You still need a friend, though. We could be best friends. Verna is starting to get on my nerves. I'd like a proper best friend.'

So would I, Ruby thought, but I don't want my best friend to be Doris Spinks. She started again on the tacking stitch. Her thread had looped and tangled, and now there was a knot in it.

'You cut a piece that was too long,' Doris said triumphantly.

Feeling as if her life couldn't get much worse, Ruby unpicked the tacking again.

Doris had been Ruby's best friend for three weeks now, and as usual she was waiting for Ruby at the school gate. Because Doris lived in the town, she nearly always arrived at school early.

'Hello, Ruby! I've got something real good for you today,' she said.

Ruby didn't want to, but she stopped to talk to Doris while May and Bee went off to meet their own best friends. Bee's special friend was Anthea Hartwig, and everybody called them Ant and Bee.

If you have a nickname, that means people like you, Ruby thought, as she half-listened to Doris complaining about somebody who'd been mean to her. At her old school her friends had called her 'Ruby Q'. Here nearly all the children called her 'Townie', but not in a friendly way. Ruby felt sometimes that everybody else was a member of a secret club she wasn't allowed to join. And still nobody had returned her little china dog, or told her where it was hidden. It must have been stolen, after all.

Although she didn't really like Doris, Ruby tried hard to be friendly. The shameful truth was that she needed her. Doris was still the only person in the school who wanted to be her friend, and in class Ruby had to keep borrowing her textbooks. In return Ruby let Doris use her good Lakeland coloured pencils.

Like Ant and Bee, Ruby and Doris now did everything as a pair. They lined up next to each other for assembly. They were ink monitors together, mixing the ink powder with water to fill the white ceramic inkwells set into every desk. At the weekly Physical Training classes Doris made sure that she and Ruby were partners – throwing beanbags to each other, pulling each other up, legs locked, in sit-ups.

At lunchtime they ate their sandwiches together while Doris talked. She told Ruby that Iris Dunn was stupid because she'd been born backwards. She said that Lorna Seidel had worms. She whispered that she'd seen Betty Pfitzner and Bob Turner kissing behind the barn where the children who rode to school stabled their horses. Ruby wasn't sure if these things were true or not, but knowing them made her feel uncomfortable.

None of the other children liked Doris. 'Why are you such good friends with her?' Bee had asked Ruby once on the way home from school. 'She says horrible things about people, and she tells fibs. She told everyone that May only came top last year because she cheated in the exams. May would never cheat, not in a hundred million years.'

Most of all, Ruby wished Doris would stop giving her presents. This morning her gift was a bottle of rose scent so strong and sweet it made Ruby's nose itch.

'It was my mum's, but she said I could give it to you,' Doris said. 'Go on, take it. Wearing scent makes you feel like a film star. I bet Jean Harlow wears scent like this. Have you seen her in *Hell's Angels*? It was on in the Mount Pleasant Institute.'

Ruby took the bottle, and then wished she hadn't.

Being friends with Doris makes me feel as if I'm being suffocated, she thought. I can't talk to Mother about it. She'd tell me that Doris means to be kind, and I should be grateful. If only Dad was here!

But Dad wasn't here. In fact Ruby didn't know where Dad was. She only knew that neither she nor Mother had heard from him for a long, long time.

10
TROUBLES

RUBY tucked her cold hands under her armpits and hopped up and down, trying to warm her freezing feet. It had been almost dark when she'd gone out into the paddock with May and Bee to drive the house cows, Daisy, Minnie and Bossy, into the milking shed. Now she was watching while May milked Daisy. This Saturday morning she was having her first milking lesson.

Getting up at dawn hadn't been as bad as she'd expected. Although she hated getting her shoes soaking wet in the dewy grass, she enjoyed the cold freshness of the air, and hearing the magpies starting up their early morning warble. And when the very first rays of the sun slowly turned the sky pale gold, she caught her breath in wonder. It was the first time she'd ever seen the sun rise.

May's fingers worked in a steady rhythm and the milk squirted into the bucket, the level foaming higher and higher. Several cats groomed themselves in the sunlight as they waited for a milky treat.

After a while May slowed and stopped. 'That's it for Daisy,' she said. 'You can have a go at Bossy now. She's quite gentle so long as you don't upset her.'

Oh my hat, Ruby thought. What if I do upset her? She went to the next stall, sat on a low stool, and found herself staring into the hairy, black-and-white side and huge swollen udder of a very large cow.

'Don't pull on her teats,' May said. 'If you

hurt her, she won't let her milk down. Put your finger and thumb right at the top and then squeeze downwards with all your fingers, the same as I was doing.'

'All right.' Ruby grasped two of Bossy's teats. They felt warm and rubbery, a bit greasy. Taking a deep breath, she squeezed.

Bossy blew through her nostrils and shuffled sideways, her big hoofs scraping and clopping on the concrete floor.

'Relax,' said May. 'You're making her nervous.'

'I'm *trying* to relax,' Ruby said. 'Bossy, please be a good cow.' She squeezed again, harder.

Bossy flicked her tail, and Ruby flinched. 'I think she's getting fed up with me, May,' she said. 'You'd better do it.'

'Not on your life,' said May. 'You have to learn.'

Ruby wanted to kick aside the silly little milking stool and run away, but she gritted her teeth and tried again. At last she produced a trickle of milk.

'Better,' May said. 'Try to get a rhythm going, like marching. Left, right, left, right.'

After a while the milk came a little faster, and then faster still.

'You're good!' said Bee, who had just finished milking Minnie. 'It took me at least three goes before I got the hang of it.'

'Yes, not too bad for a townie,' May said, with her slight smile.

Ruby glowed with pride. Not too bad for a townie! From May that was real praise. She helped May pour milk into a can and carry it out to the roadside platform to be collected by the Farmers Union truck. Then she set off up the hill, carrying a billy full of still-warm milk for the house.

I can milk a cow, she thought. I, Ruby Quinlan, can milk a cow! What would Marjorie Mack think of that?

Halfway up the hill she stopped, put down the billy, and looked back over the cow paddock. The sun was fully risen now. Shining through swirls of mist, its rays fell on the dew-soaked pasture so that the spiky grass glittered like diamonds.

'Bee, it's like fairyland,' Ruby said in wonder. 'I wish Dad could see it. He told me this was a lovely place, but I didn't believe him.'

'Of course it's a lovely place,' Bee told her. 'It's our home.'

'It's not my home,' Ruby said. 'I miss my real home. But I'll always remember this morning.'

She stood and looked for a little longer. Then she picked up the billy, and she and Bee followed May up the hill.

Later that morning Uncle James returned from the town. He drove in every Saturday to collect the mail and buy a few groceries at the general store. When he put the mail on the kitchen table, Ruby pounced on it. To her disappointment there was nothing from Marjorie or any of her other friends, but at the bottom of the pile there was something even better: a fat envelope with Dad's writing on it.

Mother snatched it up before Ruby could touch it. 'Please excuse me,' she said to Uncle James and Aunt Vera. 'This is from Harry, and I must read it in private.'

'What about me?' protested Ruby. 'Can't I read it too?'

'A lot of it will be to do with Dad's business, and you don't need to know about that,' Mother said.

'I don't care! I just want to know what Dad says, even if it is boring.'

'I'm sorry, Ruby, but this letter is addressed to me. I'll tell you later if your father has any news.'

'Not fair!' grumbled Ruby. But Mother was

unmoved. She went to her room, taking the letter with her. Ruby was left in the kitchen with Bee, who was reading 'Nut Nook News' in the *Mail*'s Possum's Pages, and Aunt Vera, who was reading about the results of a knitting contest in the women's section.

Ruby waited for ten minutes, and then she knocked on her mother's bedroom door and opened it.

Mother was lying on her bed in semi-darkness. Ruby released the blind so that it flew up with a clatter, filling the room with sudden light. 'Did Dad say anything about me in the letter?' she asked, bouncing on the end of the bed. 'How is he? Has he got a job yet? Where is he living?' But when Mother lifted her head from the pillow, Ruby was shocked to see that she'd been crying. She stopped bouncing. 'Mother, what's wrong?'

'Nothing, Ruby, really. I just have a headache. Leave me alone, please.' Mother sat up, quickly gathering together the pages of the letter.

'Is it the letter from Dad that's upset you?' Ruby said. 'Is that it? Are you missing Dad?'

'That's it. Please go, Ruby. I'll be all right in a moment.'

'Have you taken a powder for your head? Shall I get you one? Or a cup of tea?'

Mother turned away. 'No,' she said. 'Thank you, but I don't want anything. Pull the blind down again, please. The light hurts my eyes.'

Ruby drew down the blind. As she left the room, she heard her mother's weak voice. 'Everything is all right, Ruby, really. Dad doesn't have a job yet, but he's...he's doing his best to find one. He sends you his love.'

Ruby was relieved to know that Dad was all right, but she felt scared and cold. What was wrong with Mother? There was nothing certain about her anymore. It was as if she was drifting away, becoming fainter, blurring at the edges. She must be missing Dad really badly,

Ruby decided. Maybe she's missing him even more than I am. But there was something else, too, something she couldn't put her finger on.

Something has happened, she thought. I'm sure of it. And Mother's not telling me.

11
MORE TROUBLES

'OH, Baxter!' said Ruby under her breath. 'Where are you? Oh, you bad dog!'

Baxter's kennel, an old tea-chest, was empty. His chain lay on the ground, and at its end was the proof of Baxter's badness. He'd worked his head out of his collar and escaped – again.

Ruby wondered how long he'd been running free. She'd been up since half past five to help with the milking, and he was on his chain then. Breakfast had been at seven o'clock sharp, as usual, even though it was a Sunday, and on Uncle James's orders Ruby never released

Baxter until after breakfast. But now...where on earth was he?

Ruby walked around the farmyard calling, 'Baxter! Baxter!', but softly so that Uncle James wouldn't hear.

There was no Baxter; and she was late feeding the chooks. Trying not to worry about her little dog, Ruby went to the grain shed and quickly scooped wheat into a bucket. She let herself into the chook yard, as usual feeling just a little bit nervous as the mass of feathery bodies surged towards her.

'Shoo!' she said. 'Shoo!' As she moved forward, scattering handfuls of wheat and keeping as far away as possible from the rooster, she saw something flicker in the stand of pine trees. When she heard an excited yipping, she put down the bucket and ran.

'Baxter!' she shouted. 'Baxter, come here!'

A low-hanging branch moved, and Baxter's face appeared, framed by pine needles. Ruby always knew when he'd done something bad, because he looked guilty. He looked very guilty now.

Ruby's spirits sank. 'Oh, Baxter,' she said. 'What have you done? Oh, *no*!'

A short distance away was the body of a Plymouth Rock hen.

Ruby stood and looked at the dead chook. At first she felt numb. Then she began to panic. If Uncle James found out, he would shoot Baxter.

As if he too realised the trouble he was in, Baxter whined and looked up at Ruby with sorrowful eyes.

'Baxter,' Ruby said, 'you did a bad, bad thing, and I'm really cross with you – I can't tell you how cross. But I won't let Uncle James shoot you, I promise. He'll have to shoot me first. I'll…I'll get rid of the chook. I'll hide it. I'll bury it. If anybody asks me why there are only five stripy chooks now, I'll make something up.

I've never told a big lie before, but I'm sure I can do it if I have to.'

She found a stout stick and with shaking hands she began to scratch a hole in the ground. Baxter lay down and watched, his head on his paws.

The earth was dry and very hard. As Ruby scratched away, she hoped with all her might that nobody else had been near the chook yard this morning. 'Please don't let anybody have seen what Baxter did, and especially not Uncle James,' she prayed. 'Please, please, please!'

After about five minutes of digging, Ruby decided that the hole was deep enough. Just the thought of touching the dead chook made her shudder, but she made herself pick it up.

To her surprise, the feathers were very soft. The chook's eyes were closed, filmed with a grey sort of skin, and its head was floppy, the beak a little open. It looked almost as if it was asleep.

Feeling sad for the chook now, Ruby stroked the fine silky feathers. 'Poor thing,' she said. 'I'm really sorry.'

She put the body in the shallow grave she'd made, and covered it gently with pine needles and then with dirt.

Taking Baxter back to his kennel, she put him on the chain again, tightening his collar.

'Shush,' she said, when he began to whimper. 'You're in so much trouble.'

She gave him a hug, and then she went back to the chook yard to collect the eggs.

Aunt Flora was standing at the kitchen table, making bread from dough set to rise the night before.

'Bother!' Ruby said, under her breath. Although she wasn't afraid of Aunt Flora any more, she usually tried to keep out of her way. She was tired of being told how 'young gerruls' ought to behave. As quietly as she could, she put the eggs on the dresser.

'Ruby!'

Ruby groaned. 'Yes, Aunt Flora?'

'I see you have been to the fowl yard, and I wish to speak with you.' The old woman didn't stop kneading the bread dough. 'Unless I'm much mistaken, we have a pressing problem with your wee dog.'

'Baxter?'

'Do you have another beastie tucked away somewhere?'

'No, Aunt Flora.'

'Very well, then. We are talking about Baxter, who must be the worst-behaved dog I have ever come across. Tell me, has he ever had any sort of training?'

'Of course he has! He can roll over and beg.'

'Both highly questionable skills,' Aunt Flora said, pursing her lips. 'Although the begging may come in useful. As you know, Baxter has endeared himself to James by tearing up his towel. Since then he has dug up various parts of the garden and uprooted half a dozen cauliflower seedlings. He has destroyed several clothes pegs. He regularly frightens the cats out of their wits. And this morning – correct me if I'm wrong – he killed one of our best fowls.'

Ruby caught her breath. Oh my hat, she thought. How does Aunt Flora know about that?

'When I went for my early morning stroll,' Aunt Flora said, working away at the dough, 'I spied a hole under the fowl-yard fence. Not far away was a dead hen. Your wee dog was in the fowl yard too, and I observed that he had a very dirty face.'

'He likes digging,' Ruby whispered. How could she possibly get Baxter out of this scrape?

'James's patience is limited,' Aunt Flora

continued. 'He has taken in this dog – who is, I am sure, a perfectly nice dog – as a matter of charity. The problem is that perfectly nice town dogs, when let loose in the country, can be a great menace.'

Ruby swallowed. 'If you tell Uncle James about...about the chook,' she said, 'he'll take Baxter out and shoot him.'

'Correct,' said Aunt Flora. 'There's no place on a farm for a dog that misbehaves.' She floured her dough, turned it over, and thumped it down. 'Where is the body now?' she asked. 'I presume you didn't leave it in plain view?'

'I buried it. Not very deep, though, because the dirt was so hard.'

'I see,' Aunt Flora said. 'Well now. We can leave the fowl there, and risk it being scratched up by one of its sisters. Or we can turn this sad event to our advantage.'

'Advantage?'

'Indeed, yes. As far as I'm concerned, that

fowl died very recently as the result of an unfortunate accident. And if we prepare her for the pot, there will be happy faces around the table at Sunday dinner.' She looked at the clock on the mantelpiece. 'We have plenty of time. Vera plans to go to church this morning, and no doubt James and the bairns will go with her. You, however, will stay behind. You will be helping me.'

Ruby looked at her, astonished. Aunt Flora was what Dad would call 'a good egg'! She could hardly believe her luck. 'Thank you, Aunt Flora.'

'No need to thank me. We've saved Baxter, for the time being. But he's not the only problem around here.'

Ruby flinched as Aunt Flora's eyes bored into her. Now what?

'You and May should be friends, but you are about as close as your dog and that scruffy old cat he keeps trying to kill. Gaf is its name,

I believe.' She spread a damp tea towel over the bread dough. 'What's going on?'

Ruby didn't want to talk about May. 'We get along all right,' she said.

'No, you don't. And then there's your mother. She's not coping.'

'She's missing Dad.'

Aunt Flora shook her head. 'It's more than that. She's not built for heavy weather, that one. You and I are a pair: we'll not sink in rough seas. But your mother's different. Keep an eye on her.'

'Yes, Aunt Flora.' Ruby turned to leave, but the old woman called her back. 'You're not off the hook yet, lassie. Fill the stockpot with water and put it on to boil. It's time you learned how to dress a bird for the table.'

'Dress...a bird?'

'Dear Lord above, these town children know nothing.' Aunt Flora shook her head. 'You don't have to dress it up in frilly drawers and put a pinny on it. I'm talking about plucking and gutting and the proper use of a sharp knife. Get along, now, and bring that murdered fowl to me before anybody finds out what we're up to.'

With lots of potatoes and onions and boiled cabbage, there was just enough roast chicken to go around. Uncle James enjoyed it so much that he asked for a second helping, but to Ruby it tasted like earth and feathers. She noticed with a stab of worry that Mother asked for only the smallest portion, and then ate hardly any of it.

'I wonder why the chook died,' Bee said. 'None of them were sick, Ruby, were they?'

'Who cares?' said Walter. 'I can't remember when we last had chicken for Sunday dinner.'

'I hope it didn't have fowl pest,' said May.

'Nonsense,' Aunt Flora said. 'I had a good look at that bird before I set Ruby to plucking it, and there was not a thing wrong with it. I'd say it died of fright. Maybe it saw a fox. Maybe a pine cone dropped on its head.'

'I've got the wishbone!' Bee cried, holding it up. 'Pull it with me, Ruby?'

Ruby gripped one half of the bone with her little finger. As she did, she remembered sharing the wishbone with Dad, last Christmas. A lifetime ago.

There was a crack as the two halves of the bone snapped apart.

'I win!' Ruby said.

'Lucky!' said Bee. 'Close your eyes and make a wish!'

Oh, there's so much to wish for, Ruby thought. I wish Baxter would stay out of trouble. I wish May and I could be friends. I wish I knew where Dad was, and I wish Mother would stop being sad. Most of all,

I wish Mother and Dad and I could all be together again, just like we used to be.

'Well?' said May.

I'm going to wish for all those things, Ruby decided. Why not?

She closed her eyes...

by Penny Matthews

My great-grandfather on my father's side was a farmer in Somerset, England. In 1856 he emigrated to South Australia, making his home in a beautiful place called Eden Valley. One of his nine children was my grandfather. He was a farmer, too, and so was my father. My brother and I grew up on the family farm. Its paddocks and orchards, its gum trees and its winding creek were our playground.

I loved the little local school I went to for seven years, but when I was twelve I had to leave home to go to a different school. Unlike Ruby, who moves from the city to the country, I moved from the country to the city. I live in the city now, but I still think of Eden Valley as home.

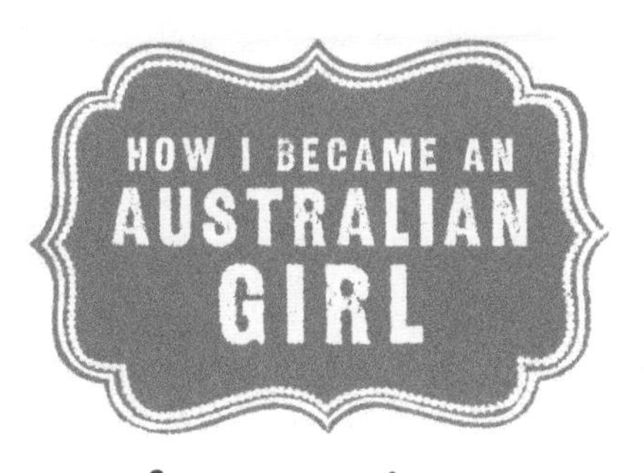

by Lucia Masciullo

I was born and grew up in Italy, a beautiful country to visit, but also a difficult country to live in for new generations.

In 2006, I packed up my suitcase and I left Italy with the man I love. We bet on Australia. I didn't know much about Australia before coming - I was just looking for new opportunities, I guess.

And I liked it right from the beginning! Australian people are resourceful, open-minded and always with a smile on their faces. I think all Australians keep in their blood a bit of the pioneer heritage, regardless of their own birthplace.

Here I began a new life and now I'm doing what I always dreamed of: I illustrate stories. Here is the place where I'd like to live and to grow up my children, in a country that doesn't fear the future.

THE Great Depression caused poverty and unemployment all over Australia, but life could be a bit easier for country people.

Farmers were used to surviving bad seasons. They grew their own fruit and vegetables, kept chickens for eggs and cows for milk, and trapped rabbits for their meat and skins. Women baked bread, bottled fruit, and sewed and mended clothes. Men were experts at everything from fixing broken-down cars to curing a sick animal.

But life was still hard. Most farms had no mains electricity, water or sewage. Baths were a weekly event. Water was precious, and very often the whole family used the same bathwater, the cleanest person in first, the dirtiest in last.

Quite a few people had cars, but many still rode horses or travelled in horse-drawn buggies. If schoolchildren needed to go to a sporting event in another town, they were packed onto the back of a farmer's truck. No seatbelts then!

Country towns were busy centres, with a general store, a school, a church, a pub, a town hall or institute, and a motor garage that sometimes doubled as a blacksmith's shop for shoeing horses. A doctor from a larger town might give weekly consultations, using somebody's front room as his surgery.

Church attendance, school activities and sporting competitions brought families together. Neighbours were willing to help each other, and a strong sense of community helped country people through the worst times.

An Aussie Icon

In 1921 an artist named James Bancks created a comic strip, 'Us Fellers', for the 'Sunbeams' pages of the Sydney *Sunday Sun*. It described the adventures of a cheeky red-headed boy called Ginger Meggs, and because it helped to lift people's spirits it was especially popular during the years of the Depression.

Sunbeams annuals featuring Ginger and his mates were published from 1924 to 1959. This is the cover for 1931.

LIVING THROUGH THE DEPRESSION

During the years of the Great Depression (roughly 1929 to 1939), people made the best of what they had, recycling, making and mending.

Small articles of furniture like bedside cupboards or kitchen cabinets could be made from kerosene tins or tea-chests. Wooden cotton reels made good doorknobs and drawer-pulls.

Bed sheets that were badly worn in the middle were cut in half lengthwise, turned 'sides to middle' and stitched up again so the worn bits were on the outside. When they wore out again, the last good bits were turned into pillow cases or handkerchiefs.

Cotton flourbags could be washed and used as baby nappies or tea-towels, or made into underwear or children's clothes.

Shrunken or worn-out jumpers were never thrown out. The wool would be unravelled, steamed to get rid of the crinkles, and then knitted up again into something new.

And for Christmas and birthdays children were given hobby-horses, doll cradles and pull-along toys handmade from scraps of wood.

A girl like me in a time gone by

Want to find out more?

Turn the page for a
sneak peek at Book 3

School Days for Ruby

FROM CHAPTER 1

EMPIRE DAY

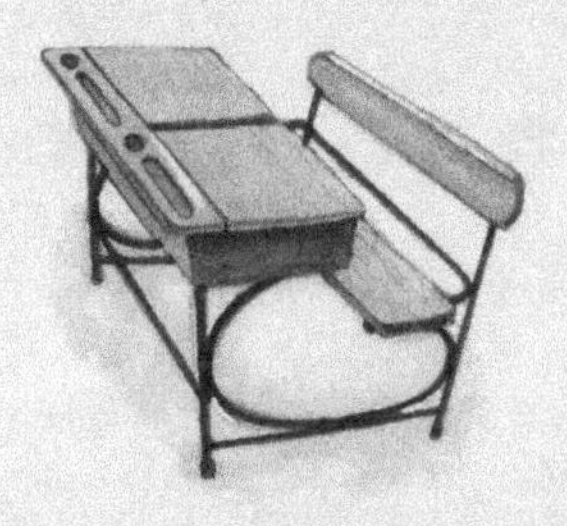

RUBY Quinlan didn't feel a bit like herself today. This was partly because she was wearing a black woollen shawl, a white apron, and a long skirt she'd made out of two sugarbags. It was also because half an hour ago she had arrived at her little country school in Uncle James's creaky old Ford, squashed into the back seat with her cousins May and Bee Cameron. Usually the three of them walked to school, and it felt strange to make the trip in just fifteen minutes, instead of nearly an hour.

The school wasn't much like itself either. Since yesterday everybody had been preparing it for the Empire Day celebrations.

Now the rows of chairs in the schoolyard were almost all occupied by parents and friends and children too young to go to school. Among all the hats Ruby could see her Aunt Vera's awful old orange cloche. Her own mother wouldn't be seen dead in a hat like that! Mother loved fashionable clothes and pretty things. But times were hard, and money was so short at Kettle Farm that everybody wore old clothes or hand-me-downs.

Empire Day was a very special day, and this year it was even more special because it was being celebrated on the last day of first term. It would be followed by Cracker Night, to be held on the Mount Pleasant showgrounds, and after that the May holidays would begin. Ruby couldn't wait.

For the last few weeks their teacher,

Mr Miller, had been teaching them about the history of Great Britain and the British Empire. Ruby was proud to be Australian, but when she looked at the big world map on the back wall of the classroom, she couldn't help feeling proud to be British, too. The map showed all the countries of the Empire in pink. Ruby knew that more than a quarter of the Earth's surface was pink, and that was why people could truthfully say that the sun never set on the British Empire.

The main Empire Day event was the schoolchildren's fancy-dress parade. While the children paraded, their costumes would be judged by Mrs Miller and the local Member of Parliament, who was the invited important guest.

Ruby felt pent-up bubbly, like a bottle of lemonade just before somebody took out the stopper. She loved dressing up, and she'd had fun putting her Irish costume together.

She'd stitched the skirt herself, and was very proud of it. Great-Aunt Flora Cameron had lent her the mothball-smelling black woollen shawl and Aunt Vera had lent her the long white apron. Ruby had cut shamrocks from green crepe paper left over from last year's Christmas decorations, and sewn them along the hem. This morning, as a final touch, she'd coloured her lips with Mother's Tangee lipstick.

Poking her head through the porch doorway, Ruby saw Aunt Vera and Uncle James talking to Mr Miller. Ruby wished her parents could have been there in the audience too, but Mother hadn't been well lately, and Dad was away somewhere looking for work. In fact Ruby had no idea where Dad was. She only knew that she missed him terribly.

Ruby Quinlan . 1931

OUR
AUSTRALIAN
GIRL

Follow the story of your favourite Australian girls and you will see that there is a special charm on the cover of each book that tells you something about the story.

Here they all are. You can tick them off as you read each one.

Meet Alice
Alice and the Apple Blossom Fair
Alice at Peppermint Grove
Peacetime for Alice
Meet Lina
Lina's Many Lives
Lina at the Games
A Lesson for Lina
Meet Ruby
Ruby and the Country Cousins
School Days for Ruby
Ruby of Kettle Farm
Meet Daisy
Daisy All Alone
Daisy in the Mansion
Daisy on the Road
Meet Pearlie
Pearlie's Pet Rescue
Pearlie the Spy
Pearlie's Ghost
Meet Marly
Marly's Business
Marly and the Goat
Marly Walks on the Moon

Meet the other Australian girls

Linas' Many Lives 1956

It's 1956 and Lina is working hard on the school newspaper. But mean Sarah Buttersworth isn't making it easy, and when Lina's best friend, Mary, gets distracted by her new television, things start to fall apart. Meanwhile, at home, Lina uncovers some dark family secrets. Living in two such different worlds isn't easy, and when tragedy strikes, she makes a mistake that causes her many lives to collide . . .

Follow Lina on her adventure in the second of four exciting stories about a passionate girl finding a place to belong.

Sally Rippin is a Melbourne-based writer and illustrator for children of all ages. She has had over fifty books published, including her acclaimed novel *Angel Creek*, and the very popular Billie B Brown and Hey Jack! series.

A FRIEND FOR GRACE
1808

It's 1808 and Grace is on board the ship *Indispensable* with her friend Hannah. The girls wonder what the new land will be like - the convict women say there are giant rats and other strange animals! Then sickness strikes the ship . . . Will they survive to reach the shores of New South Wales?

Follow Grace on her adventure in the second of four exciting stories about a convict girl who is given another chance.

Sofie Laguna, author of the Grace books, is a highly regarded and award-winning writer of several books for children. *Bird and Sugar Boy* was shortlisted for the 2007 CBCA Book of the Year Award, Younger Readers, and Sofie's adult book, *One Foot Wrong*, was longlisted for the Miles Franklin Award in 2009.

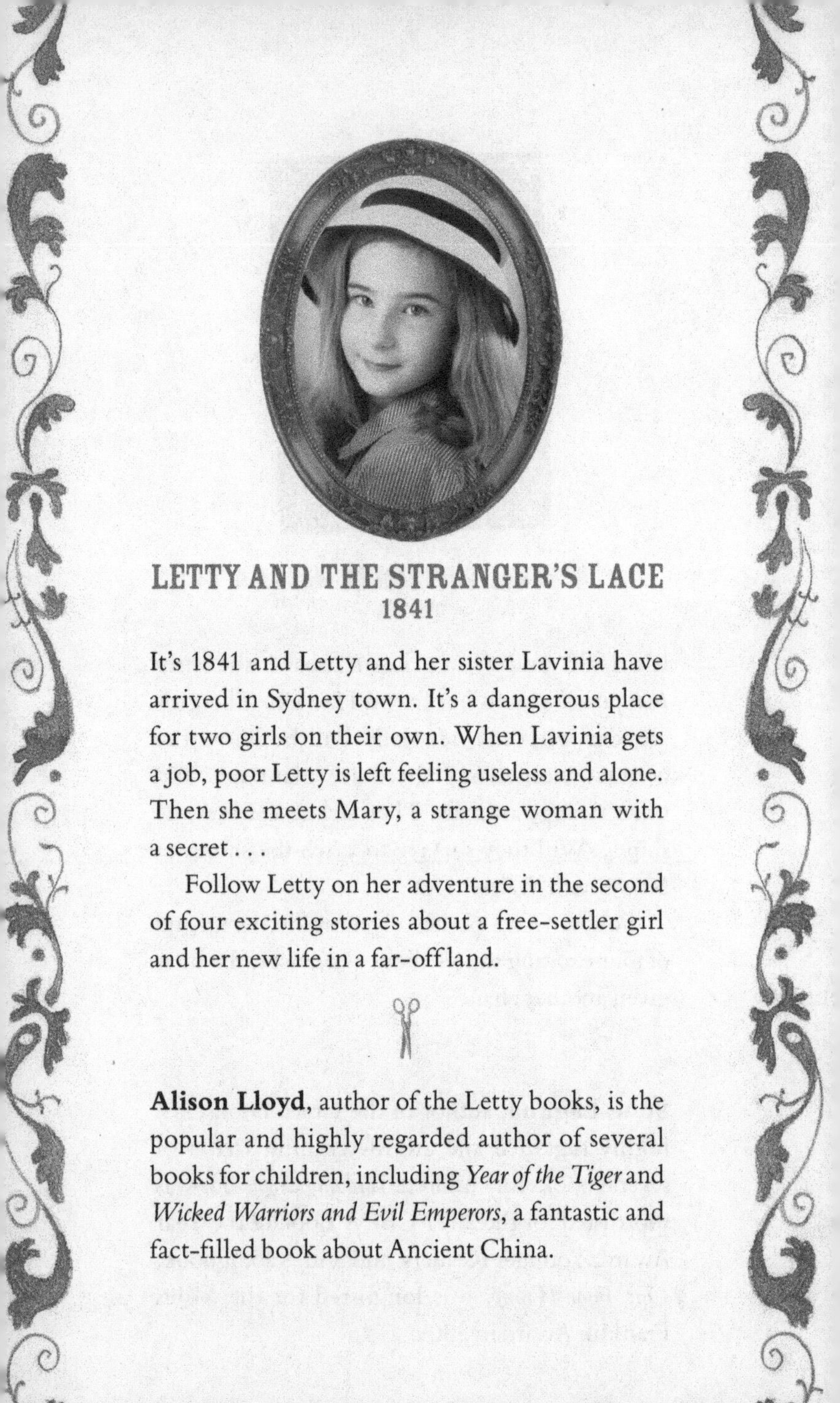

LETTY AND THE STRANGER'S LACE
1841

It's 1841 and Letty and her sister Lavinia have arrived in Sydney town. It's a dangerous place for two girls on their own. When Lavinia gets a job, poor Letty is left feeling useless and alone. Then she meets Mary, a strange woman with a secret . . .

Follow Letty on her adventure in the second of four exciting stories about a free-settler girl and her new life in a far-off land.

Alison Lloyd, author of the Letty books, is the popular and highly regarded author of several books for children, including *Year of the Tiger* and *Wicked Warriors and Evil Emperors*, a fantastic and fact-filled book about Ancient China.

Nellie and the Secret Letter
1849

It's 1849, and Nellie is starting her new life as a kitchen maid in a grand Adelaide house with her best friend, Mary. But Nellie's desire to live out her dreams soon leads to a battle with the spiteful cook Bessie Rudge . . . Can Nellie keep her temper and avoid being thrown out to beg on the streets? And why is Mary acting so strangely?

Follow Nellie on her adventure in the second of four exciting stories about an Irish girl with a big heart, in search of the freedom to be herself.

Penny Matthews, critically acclaimed author of the Nellie books, has written junior novels, chapter books, and picture books. Her novel, *A Girl Like Me*, was a CBCA Notable Book in 2010 and won the Sisters in Crime's 2011 Davitt Award for Young Adult Fiction.

Poppy at Summerhill
1864

It's 1864 and Poppy, disguised as a boy, has escaped from Bird Creek Mission to find her brother, Gus. Life on the road is hard, but Poppy is given shelter at the Summerhill Homestead. There she meets a new friend, Noni – but will Noni discover that Poppy is not who she says she is? And will Poppy find Gus before they lose each other forever?

Follow Poppy on her adventure in the second of four stories about a Gold Rush girl who dreams of a better life.

Gabrielle Wang, author of the Poppy books, is a much loved writer for young people. Gabrielle's recent books include her bestselling Young Adult novel, *Little Paradise*, and the very popular *Ghost in My Suitcase*, which won the 2009 Aurealis Award for young fiction.

Rose on Wheels

1900

It's 1900, and Rose feels that Aunt Alice is the only one who understands her. But now it looks as if Aunt Alice is going to live in Adelaide, leaving Rose with a dreadful new governess, Miss Higginbottom! Can Rose stop Aunt Alice leaving Melbourne? And has her chance of going to school gone forever?

Follow Rose on her adventure in the second of four stories about a Federation girl who's determined to do things her way!

Sherryl Clark, author of the Rose books, is a prolific and popular writer for children. Sherryl's most recent Puffin book is *Motormouth*, a companion volume to *Sixth Grade Style Queen (Not!)*, which was an Honour Book in the 2008 CBCA Book of the Year Award, Younger Readers.

Alice and the Apple Blossom Fair
1918

It's 1918 and Alice has never felt more lonely. Her father is missing at sea, her brother Teddy is away at war, and she's not allowed to speak to her best friend anymore. Alice tries to forget her worries by having a stall at the Apple Blossom Fair. But when strange events start happening in the town, everything goes wrong . . . Will the war ever be over, and will life for Alice ever be the same?

Follow Alice on her adventure in the second of four exciting stories about a gifted girl in a time of war.

Davina Bell, author of the Alice books, is a West Australian writer and editor who works in the world of children's books. Her short stories have been published in various journals and anthologies. The Our Australian Girl books are her first novels.